Little Drummer Boy

Illustrated by Claudine Gévry

Published by Sequoia Children's Publishing,
a division of Phoenix International Publications, Inc.

8501 West Higgins Road
Chicago, Illinois 60631

59 Gloucester Place
London W1U 8JJ

www.sequoiakidsbooks.com

10 9 8 7 6 5 4 3 2 1

ISBN 978-1-64269-139-9

David grew up in the inn that belonged to his family. His father was the innkeeper and his mother cooked for the weary travelers. David's older brothers and sisters attended to the rooms and stable of the inn.

David was too young to help out at the inn, so he would play and drum on the floor with a pair of spoons all day.

"How is my little boy?" David's father asked as he swung David up onto his shoulders.

"Pum pum pum!" David sang as he drummed on his father's head with the wooden spoons.

"We must find this boy a drum! My poor head can't take much more of this!" said David's father as he laughed.

David not only loved to drum, but he loved to sing, too. He sang to his mother as she cooked delicious meals. He made up songs and banged on pots, pans, and bowls as he sang.

David made music all day long. His mother loved to hear his joyful noise!

"Someday you will sing in the temple, my son," his mother said.

David liked that idea. He thought of how exciting it would be to play in the temple. It made him smile.

"Tem tem tem," David sang as he drummed on a pot.

David's mother laughed. "Your songs are very beautiful, my son. Keep singing and keep playing. Your lovely voice and your skillful drumming make my heart happy and my work light. Don't ever stop, my boy!"

A few years later, David received a small drum for his birthday. It was a wonderful gift.

"Thank you, Father," David said. He gave his father a big hug. Soon he was beating his drum wherever he went.

David would go around town and play on his drum the sounds he heard around him.

Swish-click-tum, swish-click-tum was the sound of David's brother arranging fresh straw in the stable.

Tic-tic-tic-tonk, David drummed. This was the sound of his mother stirring a pot of stew.

Pat-a-rum, pat-a-rum, pat-a-rum was how David imitated the sound of the donkeys and carts that passed by on the road.

David sang about the people who came to the inn. He sang about the horses in the stable. He even sang about his family.

One day, David's father gathered everyone together. "We are going to be very busy," he said. "Caesar Augustus declared that a count will be taken of all the families in all of the towns."

"But why will that make us busy?" David asked.

"People will come to be counted," his father said. "They will need a place to stay during that time."

Just as David's father thought, they were very busy at the inn. There was lots of work for everyone to do.

David's mother cooked more food than ever. David's brothers and sisters were cleaning the rooms and stable all the time. Each morning, David's father was welcoming more people into the inn. Soon the inn was very full.

Late one night, there was a knock on the door. It was a young man and his wife who sat atop a donkey.

The couple was looking for a place to stay for the night, but there was no room left at the inn.

David's father was a kind man, and knew that these weary travelers were in need of a place to stay.

He remembered there was some room in the stable.

"You can stay in the stable," David's father said. "It's not a room, but it will be warm and dry."

The young couple thanked David's father for his kindness. Then they walked with the donkey into the stable.

David was excited about the young couple staying in the stable and ran to tell his mother.

David found her in the kitchen and began to sing a song. "Come and see, come and see, there's two people with a donkey! Pum-pa-rum!" he sang.

David's mother prepared some dinner for the young and tired couple. When she returned from the stable, she told David and the rest of the family that the woman was going to have a baby soon.

The next morning, David helped his mother carry some more food to the man and his wife.

"The young woman in the stable had her baby last night," she told him.

"Really?" David was surprised.

"The baby is the King of Kings, they say," his mother whispered. "People are traveling great distances to see the newborn baby."

They walked into the stable and David was amazed to see how many people were there to see the baby. It was so crowded that David couldn't see the newborn at all. After he and his mother dropped off breakfast, they went back inside the inn.

David looked sad.

"What's wrong?" asked David's father.

David said he was sad he didn't get to see the King of Kings.

"Don't worry," said David's father. "We can see him tonight."

"Maybe you can play your drum and sing for him," suggested David's mother.

David liked that idea.

Later that night, David took his drum and went with his family to the stable to see the new baby. The young couple welcomed David and his family.

The stable was still crowded with lots of visitors to see the King of Kings. David stood at the back of the stable and began to play his song for the baby. "A baby born into the world. They bring gifts and come from afar. Just to see the boy who is king."

Everyone in the stable stopped to hear David's song. They moved to the side and cleared a path for the little drummer boy.

He walked up to the baby and continued to sing as he played his drum. "Little baby, I, too, come to visit you. But I do not have a gift to leave."

The newborn baby smiled as David finished his song.

"The only gift I can give is the sound of my drum and this song."

The baby's mother and father smiled as their child, the King of Kings, fell asleep to the sound of the little drummer boy.